First U.S. Edition   2 3 4 5 6 7 8 9 10
Library of Congress Cataloging in Publication
Data was not available for publication of this book, but can be obtained
from the Library of Congress.
Badger's Bring-Something Party. ISBN 0-588-14082-3 rte.
Library of Congress Catalog Card Number 94-77456.

Printed in Italy

Badger's
Bring Something Party

Story by Hiawyn Oram • Pictures by Susan Varley

Lothrop, Lee & Shepard Books

New York

Badger was giving a party. Bat brought the invitations.

"Oh, do look," said Field Mouse, reading hers. "It's a Bring Something Party."

"A Bring Something Party!" said Hedgehog. "What a good idea."

"I'll take fairycakes," said Squirrel. "I'm good at those."

"I'll take elderberry juice," said Stoat. "I've got crates."

Mole felt very grumpy. He didn't like the sound of a Bring Something Party at all.

He went to find Badger.

"Thanks for the invitation," he said, "but I won't be able to come. I haven't got anything to bring, and I'm too busy building my new house to make anything."

"Oh dear," said Badger. "Hmm. Oh dear, oh hmm. Well, I suppose you could just bring yourself."

"Just myself?" said Mole.

"Yes," said Badger. "I mean, everyone else will be bringing something, but yes…um, ur…if you don't mind, just bring yourself."

So Mole went to the party without anything, just himself. His muddy, unwashed, unslicked-down self, not at all neat or dressed up.

Everyone else was in their party best. Everyone else had brought all sorts of lovely things.

Owl had brought streamers. Rat had brought funny hats. Squirrel had brought her fairycakes and Stoat his elderberry juice. Snail had brought her beautiful young daughter.

Field Mouse had brought her beautiful young son.
Frog had brought flowers; Weasel had brought
balloons. Hedgehog had brought honey
sandwiches, Rabbit had brought some old dance
steps her mother had taught her, and Bat had
brought his accordion.

"What have you brought, Mole?" asked Hedgehog.

"Er…um…just myself, " said Mole, shrinking a bit and then shrinking a lot more.

"Just yourself?" said Hedgehog, shocked. "Gosh, everyone. Mole's just brought himself. Nothing else."

"Just himself," said Rabbit. "Well, I never! And to think we've all brought ourselves AND something else."

"Exactly," said Field Mouse.

"It's not fair," said Weasel. "We could all have not bothered and just brought ourselves and nothing else."

"Exactly," said all the others.

Mole felt about one inch high.

How he wished and wished and wished he'd thought of something to bring. Anything at all. Even that half-full bottle of sauce he had in his pantry. (Someone might have enjoyed it in a sandwich.) Even that old whizzbanger thing he'd got last New Year's Eve. (Someone might have enjoyed whizzing it.)

He crept into a corner and ate a fairycake and had a glass of elderberry juice, feeling quite, quite awful. In fact, feeling quite certain that everyone at the party was pointing and saying, "Look, there's the One Who Didn't Bring Anything To A Bring Something Party Except His Muddy Self."

And he was right. That's exactly what everyone was saying.

Beautiful Miss Snail was dancing with beautiful Master Field Mouse. It was slow, so there was lots of time to talk.

"Oh, do look," said Miss Snail. "There's Mole. The one who didn't bring anything to a Bring Something Party."

"Except his muddy self," said Squirrel, dancing past with Stoat, her nose stuck in the air.

"I hope you feel awful," said Rat, strolling over, "and by the way, I'm not giving you a funny hat because you're a Bring Something Party pooper."

"Okay," said Mole. "I won't have a funny hat. And, yes, I do feel awful."

He took another slurp of elderberry juice and a bite of fairycake, and since Stoat and Squirrel had brought them he felt even worse.

Then Badger sidled up.

"Look, old chap," he said. "I know I said it was all right not to bring anything but yourself, but I didn't mean your miserable, stand-in-a-corner-and-feel-sorry-for-yourself self. I meant your usual self. Your INTERESTING self."

A light flashed in Mole's head.

"Oh, THAT self," said Mole.

The light flashed again.

"Then everything's all right. Because as it happens, I did bring my interesting self. I've got it right here.

"Hi, Frog," he said, stepping in an interesting way out of his corner.

"Hi, Molie," said Frog. "How ya doin'?"

"Good," said Mole. "I'm doin' good. Seen any interesting dance steps lately, Frog?"

"Only the ones Rabbit brought," said Frog.

"Then check out THESE!" said Mole, who hadn't had a single dance step in his head until that moment. But now he invented a whole dance full.

"Wow, those are some dance steps," said Rat. "They're incredible. Go slow, Mole, and show me!"

Mole showed him. Soon the whole party was doing Mole's interesting dance steps.

"This is the best fun ever!" they all said before they got tired and stopped for more elderberry juice and fairycakes.

"Anyone seen any interesting party tricks lately?" asked Mole during the lull.

"Nope," everyone said, looking around.

"Well, look at this," said Mole. He put some streamers up his sleeve and pulled them out of a funny hat.

"Wow!" said everyone. "That's a great trick, Molie!"

Then he asked the beautiful Miss Snail if she'd perch on a fairycake. He put the fairycake on top of a bottle of elderberry juice and he balanced the whole lot on his snout, before it fell off.

Miss Snail landed softly and everyone was terribly entertained. They clapped and laughed and shouted, "More! More!"

Badger was very pleased. Mole had brought something really special to his Bring Something Party: dance steps that had just been invented and some very entertaining entertainment.

As Mole was leaving, Badger gave him a big badger hug. "Thanks for coming, Mole," he said.

"Thanks for inviting me," said Mole. "It was a great party."

And it must have been, because the next day it was the talk of the woods.

"Well, as it was such a success," said Badger, "I'd better give another one next week."

"I'll bring the fairycakes," said Squirrel.

"I'll bring my accordion," said Bat.

"I'll bring half a bottle of sauce and a whizzbanger," said Mole.

"And yourself, I hope," said Field Mouse anxiously.

"And your dance steps and party tricks," said everyone anxiously.

"Of course," said Mole, burrowing his new foundations and thinking how deep-down good it felt to have so much to bring to Badger's next Bring Something Party.